Rufus and Magic
Run Amok

Rufus and Magic Run Amok

by Marilyn Levinson

MARSHALL CAVENDISH
NEW YORK • LONDON • SINGAPORE

Marshall Cavendish
99 White Plains Road
Tarrytown, NY 10591
www.marshallcavendish.com

Library of Congress Cataloging-in-Publication Data
Levinson, Marilyn.
Rufus and magic run amok / by Marilyn Levinson.
p. cm.
Summary: When ten-year-old Rufus discovers that he has magical powers like his mother
and grandmother, he learns that being a wizard is not quite what he expected.
ISBN 0–7614–5176–5
[1. Magic—Fiction. 2. Wizards—Fiction.]
I. Title.
PZ7.L5793 Ru 2001
[Fic]–dc21
2001023511

The text of this book is set in 13.5 point Berkeley Oldstyle Book.
Printed in the United States of America
First Marshall Cavendish paperback edition, 2004
1 3 5 6 4 2

For Liza,
who loved Rufus from the start
—M. L.

Chapter One

I always knew my mom was different. Like Grandma and Aunt Ruth were different. Weird, some people would say, when they weren't saying worse. But *me*? I always prided myself on being your average American boy. Okay, above average in the brains department. A little below when it came to spunk. But I had a best friend—Billy, I could smack a ball pretty far (which most people didn't know since I froze up in any kind of a game), and I owned an A-one comic book collection. I figured it all averaged out. Until *that* day. The day I found out I was JUST LIKE THEM.

It happened because of Big Douggie. Big Douggie was ten like me, except he was a head taller and twice as wide. He could pass for Son of The Hulk. Big Douggie was great at football, hockey, and baseball. He also was a bully. And I, Rufus Breckenridge, was his pet victim since first grade.

It started my first day of school, when we moved to Cannon Valley three years ago. It was April, like now, and warm enough to go outside for recess. Douggie cornered me and said he could knock me down with one hand. Before I could say, "Right. You probably can," he knocked me down. He did it again the next day. And the next.

Ever since then I've been on the run. Kind of like the guy in "The Fugitive," only I covered the same ground whenever Big Douggie felt like chasing me home from school. This particular afternoon I was daydreaming as I walked—about which comics I wanted to buy next—when Douggie came flying down our street on his new inline skates. I don't know how he got them on so quickly. Mr. Faraday, our principal, had a rule: no skates or skateboards anywhere in the building. But Douggie has his ways. Probably bribed the custodian with tickets to his brother's countywide wrestling match to stash his skates somewhere in the bowels of the school.

Anyway, I was practically home when I heard Big Douggie's sweet, melodious voice.

"Hey, Rufus Dufus, I'm coming to get you!"

I turned and saw him skating toward me. I started running.

"You can't escape me. I'm faster than a speeding bullet."

I lifted my knees and pumped harder. I was in pretty good shape. Big Douggie chased me home two or three times a week.

"Hey, Rufus Dufus, want to go for a skate ride?"

He was gaining on me. Only a couple of car lengths behind.

I envisioned him dragging me down the street behind him. With a burst of speed, I raced up our walk and collapsed on the top step of our porch.

Big Douggie spun to a halt in the street below. He let out his shrill, high-pitched laugh.

"Just made it, did you? Better be careful. With these skates I'm the fastest thing around."

I turned away so he couldn't see that I was panting for breath. I was safe. Douggie never so much as set foot on the sidewalk in front of our house. But he wasn't finished yet.

"Hey, Rufus, go put your skates on! We'll go for a whirl together."

I avoided Douggie's squinty, laughing eyes. He let out a raspberry, then skated off like he owned the street. Owned the world.

Suddenly I was furious at him. Furious at my cowardly fear. I yanked up a handful of grass and weeds.

There was a gray, fuzzy, gone-to-seed dandelion in my hand. I held it by the stem and whispered, "Hey, Douggie, do a double somersault and land on your butt." Then I blew and watched the fuzz fly through the air.

Something else went flying through the air. I heard this banshee scream, and looked up just in time to see

Big Douggie sail onto my neighbor's lawn and land on his rear end.

"Help, help!" he cried in a wimpy voice.

I covered my mouth to keep from laughing. Big Douggie had turned into a pathetic blob of blubber.

"I'm coming," I heard myself say. And before I knew it, I was running to Big Douggie's side.

I reached out to give him a hand. "You want to watch those bumps in the street," I told him.

Big Douggie recoiled from me like I was radioactive. "Don't touch me!"

"Why not?"

His eyes bulged as far as they could bulge. "You did it! You made it happen! There aren't any bumps in the street."

I felt a strange prickle up my spine. In my head. What he said couldn't be true!

"You're crazy, you know that?" I shrugged like we had this kind of conversation every day. Like I wasn't terrified of him—-which suddenly I no longer was.

Big Douggie stumbled to his feet. He pointed a shaky finger at me.

"You did it, Rufus Breckenridge! You're a witch. Just like your mother and the rest of your crazy family!"

He skated away like a pack of demons were after him.

"I am NOT a witch," I muttered as I retraced my

steps. "Douggie tripped over something and—-and it tossed him onto the Petersons' lawn."

I went into the house. Spots, my dog, greeted me like I'd been gone for a month. He jumped up and licked my face, his white skinny rat's tail wagging all the time.

"Hi, Spots. It's me, right? The same Rufus I was this morning."

Spots stopped licking to let out two short barks.

"All right, all right. You'll get your biscuits."

I fed Spots and took my snack. Mom came into the kitchen. She had on one of her long, flowery dresses, and was tucking a few long hairs back into her barrette as usual. She planted a kiss on my cheek.

"Hi, Rufus. How was school?"

"Hmmmm," I said, my mouth too stuffed with a chocolate chip cookie to say more.

"What was that commotion outside? We all felt a jolt of magical energy. Mrs. Halloway jumped out of her seat and lost her spell."

I shrugged. "That was Big Douggie. He was skating too fast and came to a sudden stop."

Mom gave me a sharp look, but all she said was, "I hope he was wearing a helmet."

I remembered Big Douggie landing on his fat butt and started laughing. "He was, as a matter of fact, but it didn't help."

"Sshhh," Mom said. "You'll disturb the ladies. I left them meditating, to calm them down."

"The ladies" were Mrs. Halloway, Mrs. Ortega, and Mrs. Dalton. They came every Tuesday and Thursday afternoon for what I called their "witching lessons." The trouble was, sometimes, they forgot to leave.

"What time's dinner?" I asked.

"Six-thirty sharp. I'm sending them home at five-thirty. *Definitely*," she added when she saw my look of disbelief. "I have to, since I'm starting a new class at eight tonight."

I shook my head. "I thought you told Dad you were cutting back on classes."

Mom sighed. "I *am* cutting back as soon as Mrs. Halloway masters the good-feeling spell."

"The good-feeling spell?" I exclaimed. "You always say that can take years."

Mom suddenly looked sad. "I know. We've been working on it for years. Maybe I'm just not a good teacher."

"Or she's not a good witch."

"Rufus!" Mom exclaimed, shocked. "And don't use that awful word." Mom preferred "Empowered One" or "Talented One." She said "witch" made people think of broomsticks and the devil.

"Sorry, but maybe Mrs. Halloway doesn't have

what it takes to be an Empowered One."

"She does," Mom said. "She can cast the three basic spells, and Aunt Ruth says she's a wizard with herbs. It's just the good-feeling spell she has trouble with. No self-respecting Talented One can do without *that*."

"Hazel," a wavery voice called from the living room. It was old Mrs. Dalton, who traveled an hour by train each time to study with Mom.

"Coming, Dorothy," Mom called back. She ruffled my hair, then she went back to her "ladies."

Chapter Two

The phone was ringing when I came in from walking Spots.

"Hey, Ruf, did he catch you?" It was Billy. He asked me the same thing every afternoon.

"Nope." I didn't feel like going into the whole business of how Big Douggie tripped and fell and skated off in a panic.

"I told you, have your mother cast a spell on Big Douggie. Then he'll never bother you again."

"And I told you a thousand times, Mom only casts 'do good' spells."

Billy sighed. "What a waste of talent."

I grinned. Billy thought it was cool that Mom was a witch. He never listened when I said how boring it really was. All that concentration and meditation.

"What do you want to do?" I asked. "Ride bikes or skate?"

Billy thought a minute. "Let's ride into town. Mom asked me to return a movie to the video store. Then we can get a soda or something at Woody's."

"Sure, why not?" I agreed. "I wouldn't mind stopping at the comic book store."

Billy groaned. "Only if you promise not to stay there all afternoon."

"Ten minutes, tops."

Mom burst into the kitchen. "Rufus, if you're going into town, please pick up Griselda at P & T."

P & T was Peace and Tranquility, Grandma and Aunt Ruth's shop. Aunt Ruth sold herbs and vitamins, candles and stuff that helped people. Grandma told their fortunes.

I covered the receiver with my hand. "Mom, you promised to stop tuning into my conversations," I said.

"Sorry, Rufus. I didn't *mean* to. I just happened to be wondering how to get Griselda home. Grandma and Aunt Ruth are working late. Daddy's so tired after his long commute. Then—*bingo!*—I picked up that you and Billy were going into town."

I frowned. "Well, if you can pick up my conversations, you can whisk Griselda home on a magic carpet or something."

Mom laughed. "A magic carpet! What a preposterous idea!" she said, and went back to her "ladies."

Billy and I rode the five blocks into town. We locked our bicycles to a meter outside Woody's Sweet Shop.

"Too bad you can't do spells," Billy said. He made

circles with his hands. "Ab-ra ca-daaa-bra. Anyone who touches these bikes turns into a frog."

"How about a spider?" I said.

"Or a spider," Billy agreed. "Then we could step on it and squish it to death."

"Creeeek!" we yelled as we kicked our feet and wiggled our fingers. One of our dumb routines that made us laugh so hard, our stomachs ached.

We calmed down. Billy tucked the movie he was returning under his arm. "I'll take care of this and meet you back here in ten minutes."

"Ten minutes," I agreed, and set off in the opposite direction.

Actually, I was gone for half an hour. I'd seen two comic books I *had* to have, and spent most of the time trying to get Buddy Alpo, the guy who owns the store, to come down in price. At least I got him to say he'd think about it.

"That was some ten minutes," Billy said. He stuck his tongue out at me.

I followed Billy into Woody's Sweet Shop. Billy backed up. My nose slammed into his head.

"Hey!" I complained.

"Big Douggie's in there," Billy whispered. "With his brother, the wrestler."

My heart started to pound. "So? He's not going to

come after me here. Woody will throw him right out."

"Just warning you," Billy said. He dropped into the booth next to the cashier. In case I needed "adult intervention."

I didn't mean to look at Big Douggie, but my eyes had a mind of their own. Douggie's mouth fell open when he saw me staring at him. He turned to face the wall.

Don't tell, I ordered him silently. Don't tell anyone what happened before.

Was that my imagination, or was that a nod?

I tried to pay attention to what Billy was saying. About this great gory movie he wanted to take out, but couldn't because his mom said no movies in the middle of the week.

"Uh-huh," I said.

"Don't tell me you agree with her," Billy demanded.

"No, I was just saying 'uh-huh.' To show I was listening."

Woody himself came to take our orders. We both ordered his specialty—a lemonade with strawberry sherbet. I made myself talk about the movie Billy wanted to see, the comics I wanted to buy. I'd talk about *anything* as long as I didn't have to think about what happened to Big Douggie on my neighbor's lawn about an hour ago.

Big Douggie and his brother got up to leave. They had to walk past our booth to get to the cashier. Only Douggie made a big circle so he wouldn't have to come anywhere *near* us. Billy laughed.

"Hey, what did you do to Big Douggie? He's scared to come near you."

"No-nothing," I stammered. "He knows he can't start any trouble in here."

Billy looked me straight in the eye. "And you don't seem scared of him any more."

"I'm not."

"Why the big change?" Billy asked.

"Why should I run every time he feels like chasing me?" I got all warmed up on the subject. "I mean, what can he do? Knock me down like he did in first grade? Well, he can't. I have a mouth. I'll complain. I'll sue."

Billy reached across the table and pounded my shoulder. "That's the way to go! I'm proud of you, Rufus."

"Yeah, me too," I said.

We wheeled our bicycles down the block to Peace and Tranquility. I thought about what I just told Billy. It made good sense. I was sick and tired of being chased by Big Douggie.

Maybe I'd worked up the courage to break our routine. Maybe he really slipped and fell.

Maybe he thought I'd done witchcraft because it was easier than accepting he couldn't scare me anymore.

The strong scent of incense cut into my nostrils as we entered the shop. I started to cough.

"Rufus, dear, you must be getting a sore throat," Aunt Ruth said. "Have a lozenge." She popped one into my mouth.

"Ick!" I spit it out and tossed it into the waste paper basket. "It tastes awful."

"Full of healing vitamins," she chided.

"I'll take one, Miss Haven," Billy said.

Aunt Ruth studied his eyes. "Your allergies are going to start up any day now," she announced. "I've just the thing."

She rummaged around on one of the shelves. She opened a package and handed Billy a hard candy.

"Mmmm, this tastes good," he said.

I grinned at my aunt. "One out of two isn't bad."

My 6-year-old sister, Griselda, came skipping out of the back room. "Hi, Rufus—hi, Billy," she said in a singsong voice. "I helped Auntie Ruth straighten up all the shelves and she gave me this."

She held out the purplish crystal that hung from a

chain around her neck. "It will make me calm and wise." She giggled. "And help me cast powerful spells."

"Only if you are called," Aunt Ruth said. "Remember, Griselda, you're too young to know if you will be called."

My ears perked up. "How old *do* you have to be?"

"Oh, it varies from person to person," Aunt Ruth said. "I was sixteen when I knew. Your mother was thirteen. That's kind of young."

I let out a sigh of relief. I was only ten.

"I am so going to be a witch," Griselda said. "I know I am." She rubbed her new crystal against her cheek.

Grandma came out of the fortune-telling room followed by a very nervous client.

"You'll see, everything will work out by next week," Grandma was saying. "Your husband will keep his job, and your son will announce his engagement."

The woman grabbed Grandma's hands. "Lavinia, I can't thank you enough. You're such a comfort to me."

Grandma smiled. "We are fortunate. Right now the stars favor you."

When the woman was out of the door, Grandma kissed my cheek and patted Billy's cheek. "Hello, boys. Here to take Griselda home?"

"Oh, goody!" Griselda cried. "I get to ride on Rufus's bicycle."

"You will be careful," Aunt Ruth said worriedly. "I'll say a safe-arrival spell just in case."

A spell for this, an herb for that, I thought. Why couldn't I have a *normal* family? Suddenly I couldn't bear to stay in the shop another minute.

"Let's go! Now!" I shouted and headed for the door.

"Just a minute," Billy said. He was looking at the Tarot cards and runes.

"I'm not ready," Griselda complained. She was mooning over the crystals in the showcase.

"Yes, you are," I told her. I went over and gave her a little push to get her moving. Griselda squawked like I'd shoved her to the ground.

"Gently, Rufus," Grandma admonished.

Aunt Ruth handed me a packet. "For your father's upset stomach. Tell him to take a teaspoon in water before meals."

I sighed and tucked the packet in my jeans pocket. "Sure, Aunt Ruth, thanks."

I kissed her and Grandma good-bye, took Griselda's backpack, and led the way out of the shop. Billy and Griselda followed.

"What are you so mad about?" Billy asked as we undid the locks to our bicycles.

"Sorry," I apologized. "I don't know what's gotten into me."

But I knew. I thought about it as I pedaled furiously home. I was fed up with living around a bunch of witches. With people who told fortunes and cast spells and taught other witches.

I wanted a *normal* family. A family like everyone else's.

Chapter Three

Days passed. Weeks. I stopped worrying I was a witch. It was clear I had no powers. I couldn't work magic, even when I tried.

The way I figured it, if I'd really sent Big Douggie sailing through the air, then I could propel *anyone* forward—as long as the person was in motion.

In gym and recess, I'd zoom in on a runner. I'd try to make the kid move faster, do a somersault, *anything*. Only nothing happened. It made no difference if I closed my eyes, left them open, or blew on a fuzzy dandelion.

Nada.

Zilch.

I was a little disappointed, but mostly I was relieved. It meant I wasn't weird like Mom, Grandma, and Aunt Ruth.

I was normal. I, Rufus Breckenridge, was just like everyone else.

One good thing, though. My Big Douggie Problem was no more. Now Big Douggie left me alone. His fright wore off, but enough of it remained so that he stopped chasing me. Instead, he took to chasing after Hildegarde Phneff. He never caught her either. Hildegarde wore the thickest glasses, but with those skinny, storky legs, she was the fastest runner in the fourth grade. I almost felt sorry for Big Douggie. He had a black hole where his brain ought to be.

Billy called me one evening the last week in April. He was so excited, he could hardly speak.

"Hey, what's happening?" I asked.

"I can't say, Rufus. It's a secret! But if it happens, it'll be the greatest thing in my life!"

"That's nice," I said politely.

"I mean it, Rufus. You can ask my mom. But you'd better not."

"Then I won't," I said, annoyed.

"Hey, don't be like that," Billy said. "I'd tell you if I could."

"Yeah, I know, Billy. See you tomorrow."

Billy talked about the secret he couldn't talk about in school the next day. He talked about it after school. He talked about it the following day. Bor-ing. I was getting pretty fed up.

He called when I got home from walking Spots. "Want to go bike riding?"

I groaned. "All right. But only if you promise not to talk about your big, fat secret."

"I won't. I swear."

Billy came by. We decided to ride to the big park on the other side of town. I brought along a bat and ball so we could hit some grounders. We'd only gone a block, when Billy said, "I can tell you about the secret tonight."

"Billy!" I warned. "You promised. Not one word about the secret."

"I know. But we'll know for sure tonight. You'll be the first person I tell."

I didn't answer. We stopped at a red light. Billy turned to me.

"Aren't you glad?" he asked.

"I'll be glad when you stop talking about this secret of yours. It's driving me nuts."

Billy didn't answer. He didn't say one word as we rode through town. His feelings were hurt. Darn! I didn't *mean* to hurt his feelings. But he'd promised not to talk about his dumb secret, didn't he?

I started thinking about Billy's secret. I bet it had something to do with his father. Mr. Cameron's job took him all over the world, while Billy and his mom stayed home in Cannon Valley. Billy missed his father when he was away. I'd bet anything the big secret had something to do with Mr. Cameron.

We crossed the street and rode into the park. "I bet

your secret has something to do with your father," I said.

"Maybe," Billy said. Then he smiled, happy I was finally showing some interest. "But any *big* secret would include my dad, right?"

"Right," I agreed, grumpy again.

We got off our bicycles at the bicycle stand.

"I bet you can't guess what it is," Billy said.

"I don't want to guess." I unwound the wire of my bicycle lock.

"Try," he urged.

"Why? What will you give me if I guess right?"

"My VCR and two movies."

I whistled. The VCR was Billy's gift for his tenth birthday. "All right," I said. "You're on."

I sat down on the grass and closed my eyes. I knew how to calm my mind. I'd heard Mom lead her "ladies" through so many meditations, I could do it in my sleep.

I pulled up some grass and rolled it between my palms while I concentrated on Billy. I saw him clearly in my mind. Saw his blue eyes that were always curious, always wanting to know more. His wiry frame. His curly blond hair. Billy's secret, Billy's secret, I murmured to myself. What is Billy's secret?

A minute later, I knew.

"You're going to the South of France for the summer," I said, my eyes still shut. "You'll live in this old stone villa high up on a cliff overlooking the sea. There's a swimming pool, and tons of flowers everywhere."

"Stop it!" Billy shouted. "Stop it!"

I opened my eyes. Billy loomed over me. His hands were fists. His face was beet red. He looked like he was about to cry.

"What's the matter?" I asked. "The place is incredible! I wish I could go there with you."

Billy let out this strange sound—something between a groan and a sob. I was too puffed up with my big discovery to see how upset he was. So I laughed and said the worst possible thing.

"Hey, Billy, aren't you impressed? You said to guess your secret and I did."

Billy pulled back his arm to take a swing at me. "Hey!" I cried and moved out of his way.

"No one was supposed to know! No one! My dad said. Not till tonight!"

Billy was losing it. I had to calm him down.

"Don't worry," I said. "You didn't tell. I just guessed."

Billy shook his head. "You didn't guess. You read my mind. You're a witch, Rufus! Just like your mother!"

I was shaken, but I tried to make a joke about it. "You

wish I were like my mother. You love it that she's a witch. According to you, it's the greatest thing in the world—after movies and hot dogs."

"She, right. Not *you*! Who wants to have a witch for a best friend?"

Billy hopped on his bicycle and took off—kind of like Big Douggie did three weeks ago.

I wasn't a witch, I wasn't! I told myself as I rode home. It was just a lucky guess. Billy had no right going ballistic when I told him he was going to France this summer. He'd probably dropped some hints which I'd stored away without realizing it.

Besides, it was his own big, fat fault. He should have shut up about his big, fat secret!

I looked down at my arms and legs as I pedaled. They looked the same as always. I was the same as always. Besides, I couldn't be a witch. I was a boy. Every witch I knew was female.

Sure, I came from a long line of witches. But I didn't know a hill of beans about their ways. Like, what powers did all witches have? How did you know you were a witch in the first place?

Whenever Mom, Aunt Ruth, or Grandma talked about rituals and spells and potions, I always tuned out. Bor-ing. They involved studying and memorizing and meditating, none of which I was crazy about. Besides, I figured whatever they talked about had nothing to do with me.

I went over a bump in the road, and it seemed to jog my brain. I suddenly remembered Mom saying all witches could cast the three basic spells.

The three basic spells. What on earth could they be?

I was glad it was only the four of us at dinner. Grandma and Aunt Ruth lived next door and often ate with us, but tonight they were working late at P & T. I planned to bring up the three basic spells in a casual way. Make it a part of the conversation. But that proved to be impossible. Dad and Mom kept up this high-powered discussion about whether we should have the house painted or get new windows.

I finished eating. When I saw that Dad was finished, too, I decided to just plunge in.

"Mom," I asked, "how does someone know she's a witch-er, an Empowered One?"

"Mom, more potatoes, please," Griselda yelled. I could have bopped her over the head.

Mom served Griselda some mashed potatoes. "Anyone else?"

Dad and I shook our heads. Mom sat down again. I was about to repeat my question when she said,

"One day you know, Rufus. It's as simple as that."

That didn't help me one bit. "How did you know?" I asked.

Mom got this faraway look in her eyes. "I was in eighth grade." She smiled at Dad. "There was this adorable boy in my English class. I had the biggest crush on him. He was very shy and so was I."

I groaned.

"Be patient, Rufus. You asked me and I'm telling you. We were having an eighth grade dance. I thought he liked me. I kept hoping he would ask me, but he didn't." Mom laughed. "I used to stare at the back of his head and say, 'ask me, ask me.'" She looked at me. "Not out loud, of course."

"Uh-huh," I said, finally hooked.

"Finally," Mom went on, "it was only one week before the dance. That day I concentrated even more and said 'ask me, ask me.' I heard a voice—his voice—say, 'Hazel, I want you to go to the eighth grade dance with me.' I was so excited, I couldn't pay attention for the rest of the period."

"And then what happened?" Griselda asked.

Mom was grinning broadly now. "At the end of the class I went up to the boy and said, 'I'd be happy to go to the dance with you.' And we went."

I shook my head. "Wow, what a weird story."

"It's true," Dad said.

"How do you know?" I asked. "You weren't there."

"Of course I was there," Dad said. "I was the boy."

I stared from my mother to my father. "You never told me you knew each other in eighth grade," I complained. "I thought you guys met in college."

"Well, we did," Dad explained. "That summer, after the dance, my family moved out of state. Mom and I met again in college."

Mom came and put her arm around Dad's shoulders. "And we lived happily ever after."

Griselda clapped her hands. "What a wonderful story!"

"But Mom, getting back to the other stuff," I said quickly, "how did you know you were a witch? Maybe hearing Dad say he wanted to take you to the dance was only your imagination."

Mom shook her head. "It was his voice. It was like a telephone call. Only inside my mind. I knew."

Like I suddenly knew Billy's secret.

"I was reading Dad's mind. Reading someone's mind is one of the three basic spells," Mom said. "An emerging Talented One casts each of the three basic spells. In no particular order."

I took a deep breath. "What are the other two?"

"Propelling and scrying."

"Propelling?" That was Big Douggie.

"What's scrying, Mom?" Griselda asked.

Mom smiled. "The ability to look into water and see something that's happening somewhere else."

"You mean like in the bathtub?" Griselda asked.

"Could be," Mom agreed. "But usually it's a natural body of water. Like a pond or a lake."

"Or a puddle," I supplied.

"Or a puddle," Mom agreed. She stared at me suddenly. I squirmed and made my mind go blank so she couldn't pick up my thoughts. "Why the sudden interest, Rufus?"

I shrugged. "Just curious. You're a Talented One, so I thought I should know about it."

"You don't seem very interested in what goes on in an accounting office," Dad joked.

Mom hadn't taken her eyes off me. "Any time you want to know more, just ask and I'll be happy to tell you."

"Sure, Mom." I brought my dish and glass to the sink in record time. "Gotta call Billy," I shouted over my shoulder as I dashed out of the kitchen.

But I was thinking about scrying. Unless the incidents with Billy and Big Douggie were weird coincidences, I was two for two. The final test was scrying.

If that worked, I was a dead duck. A weirdo just like my mother. A double weirdo because I was a boy. Rufus Breckenridge, boy witch!

I couldn't imagine anything worse.

Chapter Four

I went up to my room to think. Only there was nothing to think about. I knew what I had to do—go to the pond behind the library tomorrow after school and take the third and final test. The Big Enchilada.

I had to find out if I could scry.

"Scry and you cry," I said out loud. Only I didn't laugh.

I didn't want to be a witch. Sure, they were real popular on Halloween, but not the rest of the year. People were afraid of witches, afraid of their powers, even though Mom told me that all the Empowered Ones she knew practiced only White Magic.

Witches healed people. They helped people. They were good people. Like Mom, Grandma, and Aunt Ruth.

But that didn't change the fact that in the olden days people were *burned alive* if other people thought they were witches. Right here in the United States!

Even now witches weren't high up on the hit parade. I knew *that* from personal experience. We got anonymous hate calls every once in a while. And last summer someone left a dead squirrel at the front door with a note telling Mom to put this in her cauldron.

Dad disposed of the poor creature. Mom said we shouldn't get upset about the misguided actions of some poor, ignorant fool. So did Grandma and Aunt Ruth.

"Ignore it" was their motto whenever something ugly happened. But I couldn't. I hated it when people hated my family because they were different.

Like they really had a choice in the matter.

Griselda opened my bedroom door without knocking. "Billy's on the phone. Mom said to take it in her room." She ran away before I could yell at her.

My heart did a cartwheel and landed in my throat. Was Billy calling to say he didn't want to be my friend anymore because I was a witch?

"Hey, Rufus. Guess what?"

Billy sounded the same as always. As if the scene in the park had been zapped from his memory bank.

I groaned. "More guessing games? Give me a break."

"All right, all right," Billy said. "There's no way you'll be lucky enough to guess two things in a row."

So he was putting it down to a lucky guess. I released the gallon of air I didn't know I'd been holding, and asked, "Planning on telling me any time soon?"

That struck Billy funny. He laughed and laughed. "Sure," he said. "Why do you think I called?"

I squeezed my lips together and waited. I *would not* ask him to tell me again.

Billy caved in half a minute later. "Okay, here's the big scoop. My dad says we're going to the South of France. For the entire summer vacation!"

"That's great, Billy. Really," I added, because I knew I didn't sound too enthusiastic.

Billy didn't notice. He said, "I must have dropped some hints, which is probably how you figured it all out. Besides, you couldn't be a witch or you'd know the most important part!"

"What's that?"

"My parents said you can come with us. If yours say it's okay."

"Hey!" I shouted. I stood up and jumped on my parents' bed like it was a trampoline. "You mean it?"

"Of course I mean it! Stop jiggling the phone! My mom wants to speak to your mom when we're done talking."

My mind raced ahead. "We can swim in the pool *and* the Mediterranean Sea," I said.

"And get an eyeful of girls in bikinis."

We both hooted at that.

"Let's learn some French before we go," Billy said. "So we can talk to the natives."

"Très bien," I said. It was one of the few French expressions I know.

"What's that?"

"Very well."

"Er-Rufus?" Billy sounded nervous.

Oh, no, I thought. Here it comes.

"You'd say the trip to France is fair exchange for my VCR, wouldn't you?"

I grinned. I'd forgotten all about our bet. "Mmmm, I guess so," I said, like I really had to think it over.

"Phew!" Billy said, relieved. "My parents would kill me if I gave it to you—even though you won it fair and square."

"Forget it. Forget the two movies, too," I threw in.

"You can borrow them anytime you like. In fact, let's go to the video store tomorrow after school. Dad says they have a video on the South of France."

"I can't tomorrow," I said. Then before Billy could ask why, I added, "I'll get my mom now. See you in school."

I went down to the kitchen and hopped from one foot to the other while Mom spoke to Mrs. Cameron. I heard lots of "I sees" and "it's very kind of you to ask him," but nothing like a solid, "Sure, Rufus can go."

"Well?" I asked when Mom finally hung up. "Can I go, Mom? Can I go to France with the Camerons?"

Mom smiled. "It sounds like a wonderful opportunity. We'll talk it over with Dad as soon as I get back from the Beltane conference."

"But Mom!" I yelped. "You and Grandma will be

at that conference for an entire week!"

Mom didn't answer. She took on the same dreamy look she had whenever I came upon her meditating.

Then, right before my eyes, my mother turned into a different person, someone I'd never seen in my entire life. She sat there, growing stiller and taller and more powerful by the second. Her eyes gave off sparks as they bore into mine. I felt faint. Like I was falling down a bottomless well.

"Resistance. Always resistance," she murmured.

The strange feeling passed. I found myself zonked out in a chair like a sack of potatoes.

"What—what happened?" I asked.

Mom shook her head like she was coming out of a trance. She stroked my cheek.

"I apologize, Rufus. I have no right to intrude on your thoughts. Your resistance is amazingly strong." She gave a little laugh. "So was mine at your age. But frankly, I'm worried about you."

I pretended I didn't know what she meant. "I'm fine, Mom. Just great. I got 99 on my history test, didn't I?"

"I'm not concerned about your grades. I'm concerned about you. Wondering if you've been called."

A prickly feeling ran up my spine and settled in my head. "Come on, Mom, I'm only ten years old."

Mom wouldn't be put off. "Those with the greatest

powers are called early. I sense something's happening. I've been hoping, waiting for you to tell me. But you haven't."

I shrugged. "There's nothing to tell," I said. So far, I thought.

"Because," Mom continued as if I hadn't spoken, "if you are an Empowered One, you need instruction. You must learn how to control your powers. If you don't, they'll take over and control *you*."

I shuddered. I wasn't a witch. At least not for sure. And I wouldn't talk about it with *anyone* until I knew.

"Mom, I'm okay. Really. And I really want to go to France."

Mom tucked her stray hairs into her barrette and smiled. I was glad to see she was her old familiar self again.

"I'm sure you'll go, Rufus. Unless there's a problem." Mom stood up. "But enough talking! I've a class in fifteen minutes and the dishes yet to do!"

The next day I was the second one out the classroom. Hildegarde Phneff was the first. She dashed past me, this scared rabbity look behind her glasses. No sign of Big Douggie. But that didn't mean a thing. Big Douggie enjoyed the element of surprise. That was part of his fun. His victim never knew if he was chasing that day or not.

Poor Hildegarde. If I turned out to be a witch, I'd

make sure Big Douggie never tormented another kid as long as he lived.

I headed over to the pond. There was no one around, only a bunch of geese scratching for food. My heart beat wildly as I took off my knapsack and walked toward the water.

I felt kind of weird. Anyone who saw me would think I was weird, too, leaning over the low stone wall, my eyes fixed on the water.

I was careful not to fall in. Mom would be unhappy if I came home dripping wet.

I would be unhappy if I came home a witch. I'd have to take those boring lessons. I gritted my teeth. New witches took lessons practically *every day* of the week.

An awful thought came to me. If I was a witch, maybe Mom wouldn't let me go to France with Billy. Maybe that was what she meant by "a problem."

I laughed, but it come out like a donkey's bray. There was no problem. There couldn't be. Besides, Mom forgot one humongous fact.

I was a boy. There were no male witches in my family. Not in *any* family I'd ever heard about.

I shuddered. I wasn't going to turn into a girl, was I?

I was too jittery to stay still. I jumped to my feet and ran around the pond, fast, till I was panting like Spots on a real hot day.

Calm down, I told myself. This scrying business doesn't have a chance of working if I don't calm down.

Somehow I managed to put everything out of my mind. I took deep breaths. I stared into the water. It was shallow enough for me to see to the muddy bottom. I kept right on staring. Things went fuzzy. Out of focus. Tiny ripples rose up, turned into waves. Then they calmed down, disappeared, and the water was smooth once more.

A girl's face appeared, as clear as any show on TV. She looked younger than Griselda, about four years old. Her blue eyes were filled with terror. She was screaming, but no sound came from her open mouth.

A moment later, I saw why. Thick smoke filled the room. The girl was trapped in a fire!

"Where? Where?" I demanded, then said the answer as it came to me: "385 Allison Court. Apartment 6C."

It gave me the willies, to hear myself reel off a strange address. I wasn't even sure where Allison Court was. Yes, I knew. The complex of garden apartments three blocks from here.

"A phone! I have to get to a phone!" I grabbed my knapsack and raced to the library.

Chapter Five

I yanked opened the library door. A high school kid was gabbing away on the pay phone, like he had all the time in the world.

I didn't have one second. I burst into the main room of the library. There wasn't a single person in sight.

"Help" I yelled at the top of my lungs. "Please, somebody help me! Now!"

A woman's head shot up from behind the circulation desk. I gasped. She must have scared ten years off of my life. She didn't seem happy to see me, either.

Oh, no! It was the witch—I mean, Mrs. Voss. Old Grump-Face. Mrs. Voss hated kids. Last year she claimed I'd lost a library book that I knew I'd returned. It took a visit from Mom to get her off my back. Still, every time she saw me, Mrs. Voss scrunched up her mouth, like she was eating fried toad.

She had that "eating fried toad" look right now.

"No need to shout, young man! I was busy sorting books. If you haven't the decency to wait two minutes, I suggest you leave the library."

The insides of my stomach twisted and coiled. I

didn't want to mess with Old Grump-Face, but I had no choice.

"Sorry," I mumbled. I reminded myself why I was here. My voice grew stronger. "There's a fire on Allison Court. You have to call the Fire Department."

Mrs. Voss eyed me suspiciously. "Is this your idea of a joke?"

A joke? That got me angry. Angry enough to yell again.

"I told you, there's a fire! A little girl's trapped inside." When Mrs Voss still didn't move, I added. "If anything happens to her, it will be *all your fault!*"

That did it! Mrs. Voss was grumpy and nasty, but she wouldn't harm a little girl. She picked up the phone and dialed. She said who she was and that she wanted to report a fire.

Then Mrs. Voss asked me my name. Like she didn't know it already. I panicked. Why did they have to know *my* name? My teeth chattered as I told her.

What if I'd imagined the scene at the pond? What if the Fire Department went to Allison Court and found everything okay? Now they had my name. They knew who I was.

The Fire Department punished people who sent out false alarms.

They threw them in jail.

Or in reform school, if they were kids like me.

Only I knew what I had seen! I threw back my shoulders and said, "Tell them there's a little girl trapped at 385 Allison Court. Apt. 6C."

Mrs. Voss gave a huff like she didn't believe me, but she repeated it, word for word.

I downed gulps of cold water at the water fountain. Then I sank to the floor like a pile of old clothes.

I was terrified for the little girl.

I was terrified for me.

The sound of the fire siren ripped through the library. They were on their way!

People ran past me to watch the fire engines drive by. A man came into the library.

"There's a fire in the Allison Garden Apartments!" he announced. "You can see the smoke from here."

"We know," Mrs. Voss said. A huge grin replaced her "eating fried toad" look. She pointed at me huddled against the wall. "Rufus told me and I called the Fire Department."

I staggered to my feet. "You're a hero, Rufus Breckenridge," Mrs. Voss shouted after me as I flew out the door.

A hero! I didn't want to be a hero. But I wanted the little girl to be all right. I ran toward the fire, but I couldn't get within blocks of the smoking building. It was blocked off by police cars and fire engines. A TV van was there, too. Cars and people jammed the street.

A murmur ran through the crowd: "They got her! They got her!"

There was a burst of applause.

"What happened?" I asked the teenager who had been talking on the pay phone.

"A fireman brought out a little girl," he told me. "She's okay."

"Yay!" I cheered. I threw my knapsack into the air. The fireman saved her! And it was all because of me!

I really was a hero!

I really was a witch.

I walked home in a daze. I felt strong. Powerful. Excited.

What to try next? Maybe I'd transport myself to some other place. Some other country. I shook my head. That probably took lots of practice. Besides, what would I do when I got there? What if I couldn't get home?

No, I'd better start with something easier. Like scoring a few runs in a softball game.

I thought of the little girl and grinned. Even if I never did another bit of magic, I saved her from the fire. *That* was the best thing I'd ever done in my life.

I decided I deserved a reward. I made a beeline for

Woody's Sweet Shop and a double-scoop pistachio sundae with wet walnuts. By the time I was slurping away in green heaven, I'd practically convinced myself that I, not the fireman, had carried the little girl out of the burning building.

I couldn't wait to tell Billy. He'd fall down laughing when I described how, at first, snotty Mrs. Voss didn't want to call the Fire Department. How she changed to all smiles when she decided I was a hero instead of a liar.

Then it hit me—right in the stomach. I retched. Pushed my sundae aside.

I couldn't tell Billy *one single word* of what just happened because it was proof positive that I was a witch. Billy didn't want a witch for a best friend. He'd made that clear when he ran howling from me the other day. I was lucky he decided I'd only guessed about the trip to France. I'd gotten another chance and I wasn't going to blow it.

Because if Billy found out the truth, he'd keep far away. This time forever.

The other kids would be worse. I shuddered, just *imagining* how they'd treat me in school. No one would want to sit next to me. Or be on my team in gym. Kids would complain to their parents. Their parents would write letters to the principal. Maybe they'd set up a special class just for me. A witch class. For the psychically challenged.

They'd tease me and taunt me, everywhere I'd go. In school. On the way to school. After school. In town. The kids would make fun of me because I was different. A freak. And I wouldn't be able get back at them with magic. Not with Mom telling me to "ignore them." She'd say being chosen was an *honor*. That I should only use my powers to do good.

"Oh, no," I groaned. Once Mom found out, she'd make me take witch lessons. Tedious lessons on how to meditate, how to cast spells. Five times a week.

I bet she wouldn't let me do one magical thing that was fun.

And what was the point of being a witch if I couldn't have some fun?

What I *had* to do was keep my mouth shut and find a way out of this nightmare. And I had to do it fast.

I got up and paid the check.

"What's the matter, Rufus?" Woody asked. "Don't you like pistachio ice cream any more?"

"I wasn't too hungry," I muttered and went outside.

I nixed my original plan to stop by the comic book store. But I didn't want to go home, either. I considered running away. Maybe join a circus. I once read a book about a kid who did that.

But I couldn't ride horseback, much less bareback. And the thought of swinging on a trapeze made me nauseous. Which left the real low-level jobs, like cleaning out the animals' cages and feeding them.

I shivered, as I imagined a tiger snapping at me. This was getting me nowhere. I had to do something practical.

I had it! I'd go over to P & T and read up on witches. Grandma and Aunt Ruth had all those books. Maybe there was one that explained what it was like to be a witch in a non-witch society.

Maybe it would explain how I could keep my witchiness a secret from the rest of the world.

Aunt Ruth greeted me with a kiss and a big smile.

"Hi, Rufie honey. Come to wish your Grandma a good time at the conference? She's busy right now with a client."

"That's okay. I'll just browse around."

Aunt Ruth offered me a hard candy. "Try this. It's healthy *and* it tastes good. I promise."

This time she was right, so I took another. Aunt Ruth beamed. A good sign. Aunt Ruth was treating me the way she always treated me. As her favorite nephew. Not a fellow witch.

"Do you think you can tell Mom I'm here?" I asked. "I didn't tell her I was stopping by. She'll be worried."

Aunt Ruth giggled. "Nothing easier. I'll let her know you'll be home—"

"Say in half an hour."

"With pleasure," Aunt Ruth said. She scrunched up her face and concentrated. She was contacting Mom, all right. And not by telephone.

A woman came over and asked Aunt Ruth for some herbal advice. Great! Just the chance I needed to do my research. I wandered over to the book section and hauled down a monster-sized tome called "Witchcraft." It opened to a real gruesome picture of a burning. In color.

I couldn't stop staring at the flames. At the horrified expression on the old hag's face. Or was it a man? I wondered if this creature was a distant ancestor.

An arm went around my shoulder. I jumped.

"You don't want to read that," Grandma said. "It will give you bad dreams." She closed the book and put it back on the shelf. I suddenly felt calmer.

"Hi, Grandma," I said, and kissed her cheek. "All ready and packed for the Beltane conference?"

"Just about," Grandma said. She eyed me steadily. "Do you know what Beltane is?"

I shrugged. "Sure. Mom told me when I was little. It's May first, the spring fertility festival."

Grandma smiled. "So it is. And since you're suddenly so interested in witchcraft, I'll get you a worthwhile book at the conference."

Grandma knew! My heart pounded like a jackhammer.

"After all," Grandma continued, "you come from a long line of Empowered Ones. It's time you learned about the kind of White Magic your mother, Aunt Ruth, and I practice." She waved a dismissive hand toward the bookshelf. "We don't worship Satan or practice black magic, as some of these books would have you believe. A bunch of gruesome fairy tales for the uninitiated."

No, she didn't know! I had to press down on my toes to keep from dancing. "Sure, Grandma, that will be nice. Have fun at your conference."

"Oh, I will, Rufus," Grandma said, grinning. "Believe me, I will."

Aunt Ruth joined us. "You'll be coming over for dinner while your mom's away, Rufus. I'll prepare some of my specialties."

"That's great, Aunt Ruth." I tried not to make a face like I was about to throw up. Aunt Ruth's specialties looked like burnt grass and mold and tasted even worse. I'd have to ask Dad to bring food in or take us out to dinner.

I looked up at the clock. "I better go. I've lots of homework to do." I kissed them both and dashed out the door.

My heart was pounding but I was safe! If Grandma

and Aunt Ruth couldn't tell I was a witch, then Mom probably wouldn't be able to either.

No one knew I was a witch.

"Yes!" I cheered, raising both hands as a brilliant idea flashed across my brain. I had the perfect solution to my problem.

It was simple. It was beautiful.

I wouldn't *be* a witch. I didn't have to if I didn't want to. Nobody could make me. I just wouldn't scry or read minds or cast spells. I wouldn't use any magic—white, black, or rainbow-colored.

Then I'd be like everyone else. I'd go to the South of France and have a wonderful, ordinary life. And live happily after.

Like other people did, who weren't witches.

Chapter Six

Mom and Grandma left for the Beltane conference early the next morning. Dad got up to drive them to the airport. I got up early, too. I loaded Mom's suitcase in the car. Then I offered to go next door and get Grandma's.

Mom laughed. "You don't have to, Rufus. Go back to bed. It's only six-thirty."

"What's gotten into you?" Dad asked. "Last night you cleared the table and stacked the dishwasher. Are you trying to work off some bad deed that we don't know about?"

I didn't answer. Instead, I gave Mom a big hug and ran inside. Dad was too close to the truth. I hadn't done anything bad, and I planned to keep it that way. I, Rufus Breckenridge, your average American boy.

My plan worked fine through the weekend. On Saturday I helped Dad plant flowers in the backyard. Then the three of us went to the park and watched the ducks. We ate dinner at Aunt Ruth's. She made a tofu and vegetable dish. It looked disgusting but it tasted okay. Afterward, Aunt Ruth wanted to watch an old movie on TV. Griselda wanted to stay with her, so Dad and I went for a walk. It was kind of nice, just the two of us. We walked down our street, not saying much, not feeling we had to say anything.

My question popped out, like it had a life of its own. "Dad, don't you feel kind of weird, surrounded by a bunch of witches?"

Dad looked at me and smiled—not because he felt weird, but because he understood why I was asking.

"After all these years, Rufus, it's as familiar as my reflection in the mirror."

"But what about Mom?" I demanded. "Doesn't it bug you that she can read your mind any time she feels like it?"

Dad laughed. "She tries not to. It only happens now when she's worried or upset."

"Well, I wish she wouldn't do it at all."

"Remember, Rufus, your mother mainly uses her powers to help others."

I kicked a stone. This was beginning to sound like a lecture. "Big deal," I said. "Teaching wannabe witches how to handle their piddling spells."

"It *is* a big deal," Dad said, getting all stirred up. "Without lessons, a witch could run amok. Even turn into a fiend."

Bor-ing. It *was* a lecture. And one I didn't need since I'd decided not to be a witch.

Dad gave me a sidelong glance. "Don't you think it's time you accepted that you come from a long line of witches?"

"I hate it!" I exclaimed, surprising both of us. "I wish our family was like everyone else's."

"Like whose?" Dad asked mildly.

"Well—like Billy's, for example."

Dad nodded. "You mean you wouldn't mind if I were away from home half the time like Mr. Cameron?"

"Of course I would," I said. "But maybe Billy's family's not a good example."

Dad laughed. "Every family's different in one way or another. There are step-families and single-parent families, and families where someone's sick or handicapped or unusual."

"I guess so," I said, "but no one I know comes from a witch family."

"Try to see it from another angle," Dad said. "Mom, Aunt Ruth, and your grandmother can't help being who they are. Any more than you can help being a ten-year-old boy. That's just how things are."

I shrugged.

"One of the hardest lessons in life," Dad said, "is knowing when to accept something you can't change."

We reached the corner. "Let's turn around," I said. "It's getting cold."

"Sure thing," Dad said.

We walked back without speaking. But this time the silence between us was heavy. I wished I could be agreeable and accepting like Dad. Only I wasn't. Part of my nature, I supposed. My own I-refuse-to-be-a-witch nature.

Billy called the next day around noon to invite me to go to the movies and out to dinner with him and his parents.

"Sure, thanks," I said. "Let me check with Dad."

Of course Dad said I could go. We went to the multiplex. Billy and I watched an action film. His parents saw a comedy. Then we went to Hamburger Haven, which had the juiciest burgers in town. As soon as we sat down, Billy's father handed me a packet of photos.

"Here, Rufus, take a good look at paradise."

I looked at the photos of a stone villa overlooking the sea. "Wow!" I said. It was like a scene in a movie about a trillionaire.

It was also the same scene I'd seen when I read Billy's mind.

"I'm so glad you can come with us, Rufus," Mrs. Cameron said. "You boys will have the best time of your life."

"But Mom didn't exactly—" I began, when Billy

broke in to say there was a horse farm next door where we could learn how to ride.

"I don't know," I said. "Unless they have a real old nag that's forgotten how to gallop."

The Camerons laughed, but it was good-natured. They knew how new things kind of scared me at first. Mr. Cameron told us about the nearby towns. About the beaches, and his friend's boat that we were invited to go on.

"It's practically a yacht! And it sleeps ten people," Billy bragged, like the boat was his.

"Now that's all right!" I said. For some reason, boats didn't frighten me. "I've never been on a big boat."

"So?" Billy said. "You've never been to France before. Or on a plane."

"Yes, I was," I said. "When I visited my relatives in Washington."

We were off and at it. Most people would think we were squabbling, but Billy's parents knew we were ribbing each other. It was our way of having fun.

Mom called to see how we were managing without her. It was good to hear her voice. I wanted to ask her again if I could go to France with Billy, but I didn't. She'd only repeat that I could probably go as long as there were no problems.

Well, there weren't going to be any problems, I told

myself as I got into bed. I decided I wouldn't be a witch, didn't I? And I didn't do one witch-like thing all day.

The trip to France was a shoo-in. A given.

I closed my eyes and saw horses and yachts and villas. It was fantabulous!

The next morning I bounced out of bed like a jumping bean. I was wide awake. Full of pep and energy. Like Popeye after he downed a can of spinach.

"Oh, no!" I moaned. "Something's wrong."

Maybe some people woke up raring to go, but I wasn't one of them. Usually, Mom had to yank me out of bed. I stayed in a fog till after breakfast, wondering how I'd gotten dressed and washed and everything done. But now it felt like someone had turned on a neon light inside my head.

Griselda was chatting away to Dad when I came downstairs.

"Morning, Rufus," Dad said. "Have some orange juice."

"There isn't any left," I said.

Dad shook the carton of orange juice. "So there isn't." He gave me a funny look.

"Don't you remember, Daddy?" Griselda asked. "I took a second glass. I told you it was all gone."

"Yes, you did," Dad said. "Rufus, how did—?"

"I'll just have some toast and marmalade," I said

quickly, and went to get a plate. I felt Dad's eyes following me.

Griselda didn't notice what just happened. She went on gabbing away about the kids in her class. But I was so nervous, I could hardly eat.

I was back to being Rufus, Boy Witch, despite my best intentions.

I gave myself a good talking-to as I walked to school. Silently, of course, so no one would think I was weird. Okay, so I knew the carton of orange juice was empty. No big deal. The major thing was not saying so out loud. I was going to live by a new motto: Think Before You Speak.

I sighed. Think Before You Speak was a heavy load for someone who liked to crack jokes.

With so much on my mind, I had a tough time paying attention in class. My teacher, Mrs. Mattingly, handed out math worksheets for us to do. The problems were easy enough, but I couldn't concentrate. My mind felt like a turbo engine revved to go. Zoom! Zoom! Like I had a thousand horsepower in my head!

Then the energy seemed to take on a life of its own. It reached out to the other kids. Personally, I didn't care what they were thinking. But I found out just the same.

Big Douggie was thinking about his brother's wrestling match next Saturday.

Hildegarde was worried about being chased home from school.

Billy was thinking about horses.

Mrs. Mattingly started calling on people to answer the math problems.

"Rufus?"

I gave a start. "Yes, Mrs. Mattingly?"

She frowned like she knew I hadn't been paying attention. "The answer to number five, please."

"Oh!" I was flustered. It was a complicated problem, which was probably why she'd called on me.

I stalled while I tried to figure it out. "I-er believe the correct answer isssss—" I dropped my math sheet and took my time picking it up.

"Rufus! What's gotten into you?" Mrs. Mattingly asked in a tone she usually saved for kids like Big Douggie.

"No-nothing, Mrs. Mattingly."

"Then tell us your answer, please."

"All right." I shut my eyes and took a deep breath. Suddenly the answer popped into my mind.

"It's 378,965, Mrs. Mattingly."

"Correct." Mrs. Mattingly treated me to a big smile.

Next we had a grammar lesson. Mrs. Mattingly wrote "there" and "their" on the board. "Tania?" she said to Tania Loeb who sat in front of me.

"T-h-e-r-e-" is over there," Tania said, pointing to

the corner. And "t-h-e-i-r" is their house is on fire."

"A flaming example," Mrs. Mattingly said.

Everyone laughed.

Mrs. Mattingly wrote "witch" and "which" on the board. My stomach lurched like a sailboat in a stormy sea.

"Who can explain the difference?" she asked.

Big Douggie, who usually sat hunched in his seat like a hibernating bear, raised his hand. Mrs. Mattingly was quick to call on him.

Big Douggie turned and gave me a squinty grin. "As Rufus knows, the first, w-i-t-c-h, is a person who casts spells. The second, w-h-i-c-h, is a choice. Like, which witch has the fastest broomstick?" He let out a high-pitched laugh."

My ears burned with embarrassment. Big Douggie was making fun of me again. Hildegarde gave me an I-feel-sorry-for-you look. That made it even worse. I didn't want anyone feeling sorry for me!

Suddenly I was red-hot angry. The energy roared inside my head. It shot out at Big Douggie and shoved the big bear out of his seat.

"Wha—?" Big Douggie had this dumb look of disbelief as one foot slid forward, lifted up, stamped down. The other foot slid, lifted, stamped. Slide, lift, stamp. Slide, lift, stamp. Slowly, he shuffled down the aisle.

Big Douggie had turned into a dancing bear that didn't know how to dance.

The class went berserk. The kids laughed and screamed and pointed at Big Douggie. Mrs. Mattingly was horrified. "Douglas, get back in your seat this very minute!" she ordered.

But Big Douggie couldn't stop. He did his shuffling routine up one aisle and down another. The kids howled with glee. I watched Hildegarde. First she covered her mouth to hide her laughter, then she was laughing harder than anyone.

As quickly as it had begun, it was over. I was so wiped out, my head dropped to my desk. Big Douggie collapsed in his seat. But not for long. Mrs. Mattingly told him,

"Go straight to Mr. Faraday's office, Douglas. Explain to him how you disrupted the class. You can sit there for the rest of the morning!"

"I didn't do anything, Mrs. Mattingly," Big Douggie whined.

"You didn't do anything!" Mrs. Mattingly was furious.

"No." Big Douggie pointed a sausage finger at me. "It was Rufus. He's a witch. Just like his mother."

This enraged Mrs. Mattingly even more. "No need to blame someone else, Douglas. And no need to insult Mrs. Breckenridge." Mrs. Mattingly's finger pointed to the door. "Now leave the class, before I have you suspended from school for a week."

"A week!" Big Douggie's squinty eyes looked like they were filling up with water. But before I could make sure, he gathered up his books and walked, head down, out the door.

Chapter Seven

The Big Douggie story spread through fourth grade lunch in no time flat. A few boys got up and did the Big Douggie shuffle. More kids joined in. Soon there was a long line of shufflers snaking through the cafeteria.

Mr. Carstairs, the gym teacher, blew his whistle. "Siddown, every last one of you!" he shouted like only Mr. Carstairs could shout.

The kids scrambled to their seats.

I laughed as I watched them, but deep down I was nervous. What if someone asked me if I'd cast a spell on Big Douggie like he claimed?

Sure, I'd deny it, but I was an awful liar. I'd never convince *anyone* it wasn't me.

No one asked.

Instead of feeling relieved, I felt bad. My classmates had me figured for a pipsqueak nerd who couldn't do magic in a million years. They just thought Big Douggie had acted up a little worse than usual.

Only Billy kept staring at me, looking amazed, pleased, and suspicious, all at the same time. I knew he was bursting with questions. I also knew he wouldn't say anything in front of the other three boys at our table.

I noticed Hildegarde was watching me, too. She sat halfway across the cafeteria, grinning for the first time since Big Douggie had started chasing her a month ago. *She knows*, I thought, *and she's glad I did it*. Instead of scaring me, it gave me a warm feeling. I smiled back.

Big Douggie walked in, escorted by Mr. Faraday. All conversation came to a dead stop. I had this crazy urge to make him do his shuffling dance again. I wanted to show the entire fourth grade what I, Rufus Breckenridge, could do. But I wasn't ready to go public. Besides, I wasn't sure if I had enough magical energy for an encore. I wasn't the same energetic kid who had bounced out of bed this morning.

After lunch, our class went to the computer room. Then we worked on our group science projects. The last half hour of the day, Mrs. Mattingly said we could do our homework or read silently. She sat at her desk marking papers.

My classmates were glad for the chance to finish their homework in school, and got right down to it. Only Big Douggie sat like a lump of clay, staring at the blank chalkboard. No big surprise, I thought. Douggie didn't like to read, and he didn't like to do homework. But after his visit to the principal, he was petrified to breathe the wrong way.

I noticed two pieces of chalk on the ledge of the chalkboard. They were just lying there, doing nothing. I decided to make them dance.

A moment of concentration and—whammo!—the two pieces of chalk leaped into the air. They jumped to the left; they jumped to the right. What speed! What control! I set them spinning in unison. Like two Rockettes at Radio City.

"Argh!" The sound of horror came from the back of Big Douggie's throat.

I retired the chalk dancers. I was lucky; no one else had seen them. All eyes were on Big Douggie. He gave an impressive performance of his own as he bounded from his seat and out the door.

Mrs. Mattingly took off after him. The class stood up and cheered. I pretended to be reading because Billy and Hildegarde were watching me.

Mrs. Mattingly came back a few minutes later. She looked upset.

"Where's Douggie?" everyone asked.

"In the nurse's office," Mrs. Mattingly said. "I've asked his mother to come and pick him up."

We started asking more questions, but Mrs. Mattingly held up her hand. "No more questions, please. Sit quietly until dismissal time."

"Yay!" I said under my breath, shaking my fists

like two cans of soda. "Rufus Breckenridge strikes again!"

When the bell rang, I was the first one out the door. Kind of like old times, only this time I was avoiding Billy.

"Hey, Rufus, wait up," he called after me.

"Have to go. Talk to you later," I said over my shoulder. I ran even faster.

Billy wouldn't follow me or he'd miss his bus. I wasn't in the mood to answer his questions. Though I knew I'd have to, sooner or later.

It was a great spring day. I tossed my book bag high in the air and caught it easily. I was happy. Happier than I'd ever been in my life. Everything was cool!

Sure, I'd told myself that I *wouldn't* be a witch. I wouldn't read minds or scry or cast spells. But I couldn't help it. With all that magical energy buzzing around my head, things just—happened. Besides, I only gave Big Douggie a dose of what he deserved. After all the years of tormenting me. All the times he'd made me feel small and afraid.

Well, now I was strong and powerful. I was a witch. No, not a witch. Suddenly I knew exactly what I was.

"I'm a wizard!" I proclaimed loud and clear, first making sure that no one could hear me.

My heart soared with pride! Wizards were males. And they performed powerful magic. Like Merlin, the most famous wizard of all.

"Hi, Rufus."

The wispy voice startled me, sent me reeling backwards into some bushes.

"Oh-er, hi, Hildegarde."

Hildegarde giggled. We walked together without talking. I strained my brain for something to say. Then Hildegarde said, "Thanks, Rufus. For scaring Big Douggie. At least he won't chase me home today."

I wanted to tell her, "Sure, no problem." Instead, I opted for a low wizard profile.

"You got it all wrong, Hildegarde, I didn't do anything."

Hildegarde ignored my lie. "Do you think you can make him stop chasing me for good?" she asked. "Like he stopped chasing you?"

So *that* was how she knew. My heart swelled with pride. Hildegarde believed in me. She believed I could stop Big Douggie from chasing her.

And I could. I heard myself say, "Sure Hildegarde. I'll see what I can do. Just don't tell anyone about it, okay?"

"Thanks, Rufus. I'll never forget it." And she ran off in the direction of her house, as fast as if Big Douggie were after her.

I grinned like a jack-o'-lantern the rest of the way home.

I was a wizard.

I was powerful.

I helped people, just like Mom did. And Grandma, and Aunt Ruth.

And I didn't need any lessons to do it, either.

I took Spots for a long walk. We stopped at the park by the library and I tossed some sticks for him to chase. I suddenly missed Mom. I wondered how she and Grandma were enjoying their conference.

I couldn't resist taking a quick look in the pond. The water rippled and churned into waves. When it calmed down, I saw Mom and Grandma sitting in a classroom. They were listening to a speaker standing at the front of the room.

Wow! I'd managed to scry them hundreds of miles away. Suddenly Grandma cocked her head. She seemed to realize I was watching her. My heart lurched as the weirdest thing happened. Grandma stared right back at me! And she sure didn't look very happy.

I scrambled to my feet. The scene disappeared, but Grandma's words rang in my head.

"Rufus, don't fool with magic!"

"I can't help it," I answered silently.

"Resist, Rufus, resist," Grandma said. "Until your mother and I come home."

I brooded all the way to my front door. It wasn't fair. I was the only kid in the world whose relatives spied on them long distance. They showed no respect for my privacy. There I was, scrying for the second time in my life, and Grandma had to get in on the act.

She knew I was a wizard. Probably knew it when she offered to get me a book at the conference.

That meant Mom knew. Dad knew. Aunt Ruth knew.

My secret was no secret anymore. At least where my family was concerned.

The phone was ringing as Spots and I came into the house.

"Hey, Rufus," Billy said. "I've been calling you all afternoon."

"I took Spots for a long walk," I said.

Billy laughed. "Tell me it wasn't you that drove Big Douggie berserk."

What was the point of lying? "It was me," I said.

"Incredible!" was all Billy could manage.

I waited for the bad news to follow. When I couldn't stand the pressure any longer, I mumbled, "I guess that's it for you and me. Us being best friends."

"Are you *crazy*?" Billy screeched into my ear. "Are you *insane*? Of course we're still best friends." He paused, then asked worriedly. "Unless you'd rather have a best friend who's a witch."

"I thought the whole idea of my being a witch, er-a wizard grossed you out," I said. "The way you ran from me at the park."

"Yeah, I'm sorry," Billy apologized. "I had to get used to the idea. But after what you did to Big Douggie, I look at it differently. Think, Rufus, of all the great possibilities."

"What great possibilities are you talking about?" I asked warily.

"Think big. Think unlimited," Billy said grandly. "Mountain bikes. Free, unlimited videos. Our own yacht. Hey, maybe we could fly!"

As usual, Billy was getting carried away. But this time it was over *my* magical powers.

"Look, Billy, it doesn't quite work that way. I can't just conjure up anything I like."

"Sure you can," Billy insisted. "Look what you did to Big Douggie. You have him scared of his own shadow."

"I have to go," I said. "See you tomorrow." I hung up before Billy could come up with another crazy way for me to use my magic.

The house was empty, too empty, with Mom away. Griselda was at P & T with Aunt Ruth. Dad was at work.

I fed Spots, then I went upstairs to do my homework. Only I couldn't concentrate. I threw myself down on my bed.

Being a wizard was complicated. When I was full of that magical energy, I did things I wouldn't ordinarily do.

And it gave people all kinds of expectations. Hildegarde wanted help. Billy wanted fun and games. Mom and Grandma couldn't wait to stick me in a class so I could learn to do good deeds. Boring deeds.

I pulled my pillow over my head. This wizard thing was taking on a life of its own.

Chapter Eight

Dad came home around six, and we went next door for dinner.

"Look what Auntie Ruth gave me," Griselda greeted us. She held up a new crystal. Green, this time.

"Don't wear all your crystals at once," I told her. "You've got so many, they'll give you a sore neck."

"They will not!"

"Hello, Rufie honey." Aunt Ruth kissed my cheek. "Hungry? Everything will be ready in just a few minutes."

It was a typical Aunt Ruth dinner. First we had dandelion soup, then veggie burgers, a salad, and some broccoli. Everything tasted okay but the broccoli.

"When I grow up, I'm going to be a vegetarian like Aunt Ruth," Griselda announced.

I pretended to be shocked. "You mean, give up hamburgers and meatballs and fried chicken?" I asked. "Forever and ever?"

Griselda looked at Aunt Ruth. "Well, maybe I'll be a vegetarian some days," she said.

We all laughed.

Dad and Aunt Ruth drank coffee and talked about

some new zoning ruling in town. Griselda and I went into the den. I switched on the TV. There was a Charlie Brown special, one I'd seen a hundred times.

"Leave it on, Rufus," Griselda begged. "P-l-e-a-s-e."

"You owe me, Griselda. Big time."

Griselda nodded happily, then got lost in her program.

I started pacing. There was nothing to do. Nothing to read but Aunt Ruth's herbal magazines. I wished I'd thought to bring over some comics. I wished we could go home.

"When are we going home?" I called out to Dad.

"Very soon," Dad answered. "Be patient, Rufus."

My eyes settled on the doll collection in the corner of the den. Aunt Ruth kept about forty dolls in a cabinet she'd had custom made. The dolls were from all over the world. Aunt Ruth hadn't been to most of the countries they came from. But she said she could imagine being there by looking at the dolls.

I especially liked the Spanish doll. She had long black hair and wore a shiny red dress and a lace mantilla.

I suddenly got this great idea.

"Hey, Griselda," I said softly. "Watch this."

It hardly took any effort to walk the Spanish doll down from its shelf and across the floor to where Griselda was stretched out on her stomach.

Griselda giggled as the doll stopped half an inch from her nose.

I was proud of my little sister. She wasn't frightened. And she had enough sense not to touch the doll as I guided it across the den floor.

"Again, Rufie! Do it again!"

"Certainly," I said, bowing. "With pleasure." I had the doll turn around and retrace its steps.

Griselda giggled louder. "Again!"

"Rufus!"

Aunt Ruth's exclamation startled us both. Dad came over and grabbed my arm.

"Don't you ever do anything like that again!" he bellowed. "*Never!* Is that clear?" His pit-bull grip squeezed tighter. It hurt.

"Ouch!" I complained, and tried to wriggle free.

Dad immediately let go and I went flying. When he tried to steady me, I flinched.

"Sorry, Rufus," Dad apologized. His face was ablaze with embarrassment. Dad wasn't your manhandling type of father. He never spanked me, not even that time I was little and ran into the street.

"Your grandma told you not to fool with magic," Aunt Ruth said softly.

"I was only kidding around," I said lamely.

"Your mother's taught you magic is for good deeds," Dad said. "Use magic for the wrong reasons, and it will ruin your life," he said in this raspy voice I'd never heard before. "Keep it up and you'll lose your soul, your family—everything you hold dear."

Aunt Ruth touched Dad's arm. "Don't upset yourself, Simon."

"It's happening all over again," Dad said. "I saw the signs. Hazel saw the signs. But she said to wait until after the conference."

He sank onto the couch, held his head in his hands. "We can't wait, Ruth. Not another minute."

Aunt Ruth nodded. "You're right, Simon." She gave me a level look. "It's time Rufus knew."

A chill ran down my spine. Things were getting weirder and scarier. And real interesting.

"Will someone please explain what you're talking about," I shouted.

"No need to shout, Rufus," Aunt Ruth said. She took Griselda's hand. "Come upstairs, honey, for some homemade root beer."

"I want to know the big secret, too," Griselda said.

"You will, Griselda, when you're older," Aunt Ruth said. She led my sister away.

I felt a little self-conscious, now that Dad and I were

alone. Aunt Ruth's Spanish doll lay on the carpet. I put it back in the cabinet. Then I sat down next to Dad on the den sofa.

"So," I said, trying for flippant, "the whole family knows I'm a wizard."

I waited for Dad to tell me I was a witch. Or an Empowered One. Instead he shook his head.

"Amazing. That's exactly what he used to call himself. A wizard."

More mystery. I let out a snort of impatience. "*Who* called himself a wizard? Come on, Dad, let me in on it."

Dad's eyes held mine. "My brother, Rufus. I'm talking about my brother."

"Wow!" I let out a long breath of air. "I never knew I had an uncle. What's his name, Dad? How come I never met him?" I thought a moment. "How come you never told me about him till now?"

Dad sighed. "Partly because I haven't seen Hector since I was sixteen. He left home just before his high school graduation. We never heard from him again."

I shook my head. "I can't believe it. Nana and Grandpa never talk about him, either. What did he do? Rob a bank?"

"Worse," my father said bleakly. "Hector had powerful magic. Even stronger than your grandma's. And he used it for all the wrong reasons."

"Like what?" I asked. I had to know. It was like the time I came upon Spots killing a rabbit. It was horrible. Gory. But I had to see it all.

"Oh, for anything he liked. An expensive car. To get back at a teacher who gave him detention. Unscrupulous people found out about his powers. They paid Hector money. To do—certain favors."

My mouth fell open. "You mean, Hector killed people?"

Dad's face went white. He had to clear his throat a few times before he could go on.

"I can't say for sure. But he hurt people, all right."

Dad stopped and I waited in silence. I saw how difficult this was for him.

"Hector had a fight with his friend, Timmy, over a girl they both liked. Only the girl liked Timmy. That night, Timmy and the girl were in a terrible car accident. They both spent months in the hospital."

My throat was dry. "How did you know Hector had anything to do with the car crash?"

"Because an hour before it happened, my brother called the girl and told her not to go out with Timmy or something would happen to them. That night Hector left town. We never heard from him again."

Wow! This was more like a Stephen King book than a family story. And I was *used* to witches.

"I wonder where Uncle Hector is now," I said.

"He's evil!" my father said sharply. "I hope he stays far, far away as long as he lives."

I stared at my father, too shocked to speak.

"Rufus, I'm telling you all this, so you don't make the same mistake. I pray it will convince you to treat your magical powers seriously and with respect. To use them to help others. Like Mom, Aunt Ruth, and your grandmother do."

Another lecture. "But all I did was make the doll move," I said.

"That's how Hector began," my father said. "Playing little games, doing little tricks. He had no one to teach him to use his powers for good deeds. And so Hector fell under the spell of his own magic. It corrupted him."

"But I wouldn't let that happen," I protested. "I would never cause a car accident."

"The power grows, Rufus. If you don't learn to control it, it controls you."

I hung my head. "I'm sorry, Dad."

"Just hold on for a few more days," Dad said. "Until Mom and Grandma come home. Then you'll start your lessons. You'll find out what you can and can't do." Dad tousled my hair. "Can you manage that?"

I nodded. "Uh-huh."

Dad smiled. "Thanks, Rufus. You're a good boy. I knew I could count on you."

Dad's story about Uncle Hector got through to me loud and clear. I told myself I wouldn't upset my family again. I wouldn't use my powers *at all* until Mom came back—I sighed—and the witch lessons began.

But I couldn't stop thinking about Uncle Hector. I knew the last thing Dad wanted was to make him out to be a champion or a superstar. But that's exactly how he seemed to me—a powerful wizard, who could do anything he wanted.

I hated to think of his part in the car crash. Instead, I pictured him as a James Dean figure. Vulnerable. Rejected. Leaving town so he wouldn't have to face losing his girl to his best friend.

Still, there was no getting away from it. Hector did bad deeds. Evil deeds. Which made him an evil wizard. Like ogres and giants in fairy tales. I always thought they were made up characters. Now I wasn't so sure.

Mom said all the witches she knew used their powers to do good deeds.

But some witches and wizards used their powers to do evil.

I shuddered. The world didn't seem as safe to me as it had before my conversation with Dad.

At least I wasn't like Uncle Hector, I told myself. I didn't think I'd ever hurt anyone, not even Big Douggie. Or use magic to get something I wanted, like valuable comic books.

The trouble was, I didn't know for sure.

Chapter Nine

The next day I woke up tired and grouchy. *Anyone* would be tired and grouchy after wrestling with his quilt half the night. When I finally drifted off, I dreamed of a scary guy in a black cape.

Was he supposed to be Dracula? Uncle Hector?

Or me?

I gobbled down half a bagel and hurried off to school. It felt like old times. No sign of that magical energy. Maybe my resolution not to cast any spells till Mom got back was keeping it away. After all, it seemed to have worked over the weekend.

I can do it, I told myself as I walked. I, Rufus Breck-enridge, was in control of my life. I was running on will power.

Only it wasn't that easy. Without even *trying*, I started reading kids' minds. A lot depended on the strength of their feelings. And boy, did some kids have powerful feelings.

Big Douggie, for example. His thoughts ran to crush-ing bones and dripping blood. Mostly what he'd like to do to me if he wasn't afraid I'd turn him into a frog.

I nearly laughed. There was that old frog scare again, left over from fairy tales.

I didn't like what he had planned for Hildegarde, either. He hated her, too. Especially after seeing us talking together yesterday after school.

Billy was a problem now that he thought having a wizard for a best friend was the coolest thing in the world. All morning he bombarded me with crazy ideas. First he'd fake a coughing fit. Then, when he was bent over double, he'd flick a tiny, folded-up note to me along the floor.

"How about going to Woody's and have him make us ice cream sundaes *three feet tall*?"

"How about, when we get to the South of France, you make us 21 so we can meet girls, drive a convertible, and have a ball?"

"How about making Big Douggie do the shuffle?"

Mrs. Mattingly asked Billy if he wanted to go to the nurse.

Billy blushed. "No, I'm okay. I just have this tickle in my throat."

The fourth note never reached me. Big Douggie's paddle-sized sneaker stopped it midway. Billy's neck turned blood red as Big Douggie unfolded the bit of paper. I forgot my promise not to do *any* magic, and scanned the note to see what he had written.

"How about turning Big Douggie into a frog?"

Big Douggie let out a yelp. He dropped the note like it was on fire.

"Is that a note, Douglas?" Mrs. Mattingly asked, knowing darn well what it was. She stretched out her hand. "Please hand it to me."

"No!" Big Douggie croaked. He popped it into his mouth and started chewing.

The class cracked up laughing.

"Douglas, to the office!"

"That's not fair!" Big Douggie whined, still chewing. "I didn't write the note."

"But you read it!" Mrs. Mattingly said through clenched teeth.

"Only because Billy's been using the aisle for a post office all morning," Big Douggie said.

Mrs. Mattingly turned to Billy. "Is that true, William?"

Billy caved in easily. He was two questions away from telling everything to everyone. I had to act *immediately* if I didn't want the world to know I was a wizard.

My eyes landed on the PA speaker just below the clock. The noon bell, I thought. Maybe I could ring the bell and we could go to an early lunch.

A bell went off, all right, but it was the fire alarm clanging throughout the school.

"Fire drill!" Mrs. Mattingly announced. We stood

and formed a double line. Mrs. Mattingly eyed Billy and Big Douggie. "We'll talk about this later."

"Cool," Billy said, smacking me high five as we walked down the hall. "Only a witch could pull off a fire drill at exactly the right moment."

"Wizard, Billy, wizard. And I didn't mean to—" I broke off as Mrs. Mattingly walked by.

"No talking, boys," she said.

"You have to stop this," I hissed.

"Stop what?" Billy asked. "You're the one who cast a major spell."

I wanted to grab Billy's shoulders and shake some sense into him. "Forget I'm a wizard, will you? I can't do any more magic till my mother comes home. And I bet she won't let me do *anything* once she's back," I ended grumpily.

"More reason to live it up now," Billy said as we exited the building. "And this," he threw open his arms, "was a stroke of genius."

"You don't understand!" I yelled. "I didn't mean to set off the fire alarm. It just happened."

Billy *had* to be the strangest kid in the universe. He stared at me in pure admiration. "That's *awesome*, Rufus. Magic run amok."

It was more amok than we knew. The alarm turned on the sprinkler systems in the cafeteria and the gym.

The entire maintenance crew set to work mopping up the floors. Some teachers went to help them. Meanwhile, they kept us outside.

At first it was fun. After ten minutes, we got restless. "When can we go to lunch?" kids kept asking.

"As soon as the floor is dry," Mrs. Mattingly answered.

My hands grew clammy. My heart started to pound. I was responsible for everything. If Mrs. Mattingly found out, I'd be thrown out of school.

"Not a word to anyone about this," I told Billy. "Got it? No one!"

Billy acted like I told him I was giving away my comic book collection. "Are you crazy, Rufus?" he demanded. "Once word gets out, you'll be a hero. Big time. The kids will carry you around on their shoulders."

"No they won't. They'll think I'm weird. Just keep it to yourself."

Billy shook his head. "Whatever you say. But, trust me, you're making one big mistake."

My knees started shaking when Mr. Faraday walked toward us, but he'd only come to tell Mrs. Mattingly what was happening. When he left, she said, "They managed to shut off the sprinkler systems a few minutes ago. Mopping up the cafeteria will take a while, so we'll eat outside."

I gulped while everyone else cheered. Mrs. Mattingly called for quiet. "We'll go inside now and get our lunches from our cubbies," she said. "Who buys lunch in the cafeteria?"

Hildegarde, Big Douggie, five other kids, and I raised our hands.

Mrs. Mattingly locked each of us in her gaze. "Buy your lunch and meet us at the outside benches as *soon as possible*. Is that understood?"

"Yes, Mrs. Mattingly," we answered.

"What about getting drinks and ice cream?" someone asked.

"We'll send for that later," Mrs. Mattingly said. "Now, class, follow me."

"Well done, Rufus!" Billy whispered. He gave me a wink.

I pretended not to notice. No more magic, I swore to myself. No matter what.

The cafeteria eight was bringing up the rear, when Big Douggie made his move. He shouldered Hildegarde like he was tackling a quarterback. Hildegarde crumpled to the ground.

The five other kids gasped in horror. But since they didn't want the same treatment, they walked double-time to the cafeteria.

"Hey, what'd you do that for?" I yelled as I helped Hildegarde to her feet.

"For practice." Big Douggie grinned.

Ask a stupid question, you get a stupid answer. But one thing was clear. Big Douggie was no longer afraid of me.

Why? I wondered. I shivered, suddenly frightened. Then I remembered who I was. *What* I was.

"Leave Hildegarde alone, Douggie," I said. "I mean it."

"Suuuuure," Big Douggie drawled. "When it snows in July."

I bit my lip. "Wanna be a frog for a day or two?"

I watched him turn pale. Then he grinned again. "You won't be doing any more magic, Rufus Dufus. Your mommy won't let you."

My face turned red. So that was it! Big Douggie heard me talking to Billy. My head started to buzz as the magical energy came to life.

"I'll do what has to be done," I said stiffly.

That made Douggie laugh. "Like setting off a fire drill? Wait till I tell Mrs. Mattingly."

*

"Thanks, Rufus," she whispered, and hurried away.

No magic, I reminded myself. I'd have to bluff my way out of this.

"Mrs. Mattingly won't believe I had anything to do

with the fire drill," I said. "Like she didn't believe I had you do the Big Douggie Shuffle yesterday."

Big Douggie scratched his head. Wood burned. The big lug was thinking.

"Maybe not," he finally said thoughtfully. "But after I plaster the school with flyers saying 'Rufus is a witch,' you'll be surprised at how many people will believe it."

I stared up at Big Douggie. His brains were tucked away, but they were there, all right. Because he'd managed to come up with the one thing I dreaded most: exposure.

I was desperate. "Don't think I won't turn you into a frog," I lied.

Big Douggie laughed. "Your mother wouldn't let you. She only does good magic."

How did he know that? I was starting to panic. "You'll see what I can do!" I yelled.

"I *know* what you can do."

It was the first sign of respect Big Douggie had ever shown me. Had ever shown *anybody*. I was too dumbfounded to speak.

"What I was thinking," Big Douggie continued, "was maybe you could do me a favor."

"Favor?" I echoed. The word sounded dirty. Of course. Dad's story of Uncle Hector.

"Just a little favor," Big Douggie said, "and I'll leave

Hildegarde alone."

"You will?" I asked.

It was the wrong thing to say. Big Douggie slapped me on the back. It was a powerful slap, but meant in a friendly way. "Sure I will, Rufus."

He looked around, like he was worried someone might hear what he was about to tell me. Then he started mumbling.

"What? Talk louder," I said.

His beefy mitt of a hand pulled me closer. He mumbled again, but this time I heard him.

"It's like this, Rufus. My swing isn't connecting. Last Little League game I was 0 for 3. *Not one single hit.*" His eyes sank to the ground. "You gotta get me out of this slump."

I pulled free of his death grip. "How? I'm not a baseball clinic. I don't know how to make you hit the ball."

Douggie tapped his head. "Think, Rufus. Your magic. It can make me connect with the ball. At the tryouts in gym this afternoon."

I stared at him like he was crazy. "What tryouts, Douggie? We'll do some warm-up exercises, then play our usual softball game."

Douggie's sausage finger poked me in the ribs. "That's all you know, Mr. Math Genius, who always gets 100 on a test. And *that's* what you're supposed to think. But I got it from my brother, who got it from *his* coach that today they're picking the players for the Cannon Valley All-Star Game."

I shrugged. "So?"

Big Douggie gave me his squinty smile. "Make it so I hit at least a double, and I act like Hildegarde doesn't exist."

"Do you swear?"

Big Douggie held his hand to his heart. "I swear."

"You won't change your mind and ask me for another favor?"

"I swear number two." Big Douggie shook his head in disbelief. "Just one little double, Rufus, and I'll be back in stride."

All this swearing didn't make me feel any better. Sure, I'd be helping Hildegarde like I'd promised, but at the expense of doing Big Douggie a favor. A *magical spell* of a favor. Something I told myself I wouldn't do till Mom came home.

I tried stalling. "Er, Douggie, maybe we should wait a few days. This magic stuff is new to me. It doesn't always work so great."

"Sure it does." Big Douggie's eyes clamped onto mine. "This afternoon, Rufus. It's gotta be this afternoon."

May as well get it over with, I thought, and gave a

little nod.

Big Douggie whooped as he leaped into the air. He threw an arm around my shoulder and squeezed.

"Let's get lunch before Mattingly comes after us," he said. He didn't let go of me till we got to the cafeteria.

It was awful. Anyone seeing us would get the impression we were the best of friends.

Chapter Ten

"What took you so long?" Billy demanded as soon as I came outside with my lunch.

"Big Douggie and I had a chat."

Billy whistled. "You're kidding."

"I wish," I said, and told him what happened.

When I was done, Billy said, "There's only one way to deal with this. Turn him into a frog." He started to laugh.

I pounded Billy on the back. Hard.

"Ow," he complained. "What did you do that for?"

"For turning everything into a joke. For not understanding how hard all this is for me."

"Hard?" Billy's blue eyes opened wide. "The way I see it, you have the world at your feet. You can do whatever you like."

"Yeah. Sure," I said sarcastically. "If that's true, how come Big Douggie is making me do him a favor?"

Billy thought, then he nodded. "I guess he's not as dumb as we thought."

"Exactly. He doesn't get good grades, but he knows other kinds of things." I sighed. "And he's still pushing me around. Now he's cashing in on my magic."

Billy put his hand on my shoulder. "Look at it this way, Rufus. You're helping Hildegarde."

"Yeah," I conceded. "We have to look on the bright side of things."

We had a short history lesson. Then we lined up for gym. I looked over at Big Douggie, but he was staring straight ahead. He'd been behaving himself ever since our little talk. I guess he didn't want to remind Mrs. Mattingly that he was supposed to go to the office for not handing over Billy's note. I bet Mrs. Mattingly remembered and decided to forget the whole business. Teachers sometimes surprised you that way.

Our class and Mrs. Baskin's class went outside. The playing field was just past the kindergarten playground. You could see it from our windows.

It was obvious something was up. The two gym teachers from the other elementary schools were in a huddle with Mr. Carstairs. They all carried clipboards. Instead of doing roll call, Mr. Carstairs asked the teachers who was absent. Then he cupped his hands like a bullhorn.

"Listen up, people. We're going to skip our warm up today and divide into four teams for two soft ball games. Instead of choosing up the usual way, I'll pick the captains and the teams."

One sweep of his head, and he caught all fifty-four of us in his scowl. "No talking, or you might not hear which team you're on. Believe me, you *don't want that to happen.*"

I shivered. Mr. Carstairs had that kind of effect.

He named the four captains, then called the rest of us in alphabetical order, so I was one of the first. I waited under the tree with Team A. I closed my eyes and took a deep breath.

Please let me have enough magic, I said silently, to make Big Douggie hit a double so he'll leave Hildegarde alone and never ask me for another favor as long as he lives.

I took another deep breath. Then I opened my eyes and smiled. All that energy crackling and popping in my head meant the magic was building up to full force.

Big Douggie was on Team C. They took their positions in the field like we were doing. Great! Perfect! The two games were close enough so I could keep an eye on things, make my move when I had to.

Deep in the outfield, my confidence took a dive. The nerves in my stomach twang like guitar strings.

What if I couldn't pull it off?

What if what I was doing was illegal? I felt bad, giving Big Douggie this advantage. Lots of kids were *dying* to play in the All-Star Game.

But Douggie was *good*, I told myself. He was the best hitter in the grade. He deserved to be in the game. Everyone knew that. Besides, he wasn't being greedy. He didn't ask me for a home run. Just a measly double.

Come on, Rufus, you can manage a *double*, I spurred myself on. Think of it this way: you're helping out a guy in a slump. Even if it is Big Douggie.

Then I tackled what was worrying me the most. I reminded myself that *no one* would guess in a million years that I had anything to do with Big Douggie's double.

Big Douggie wouldn't tell. Billy wouldn't tell. And if Hildegarde guessed, she wouldn't tell.

I was home free.

"Catch it, Rufus! Catch it!"

I was so busy worrying, I had no time to agonize over the ball coming at me. I raised both hands and caught it neatly. Then I pulled back my arm like the professionals do and threw it to the pitcher.

My team cheered. "Atta boy, Rufus," Mr. Carstairs called as he scribbled in his clipboard.

I grinned. I, Rufus Breckenridge, who never snagged fly balls, who never made outs, had just caught one deep in left field. And it wasn't the magic, either. Just plain reflex action. I'd been too worried about Big Douggie's double to have my usual nervous dropsies.

I stayed alert, but the ball didn't come anywhere near me again. A player got to first. He tried to steal, and got caught. Two outs. Hildegarde came to bat. She bounced a double. The next kid up got on base and Hildegarde came home. Billy made a single. Their team scored two more runs. Then a batter popped up and we changed sides. Big Douggie's team, I noticed, was still out there fielding.

They sure took their time about it. My team made three runs and two outs when Big Douggie's team finally got up to bat. I gave a sigh of relief. Gave another one when I saw Big Douggie was first to bat. Finally! He'd have his double before our team went back to the field.

"Rufus, you're up," Jeff Stein, Team A's captain called to me.

"I am? Do I have to?"

Some of my teammates laughed. I couldn't blame them. It was a dumb thing to say.

"Move it, Rufus," Jeff barked. "And try to get on base for a change."

More laughter. Everyone knew I always went down swinging.

I grabbed a bat and took a few swings over home plate. Big Douggie and I were about ten feet apart and facing in opposite directions. He turned and gave me a wink.

It didn't make me feel any better.

"Strike one!" Mrs. Mattingly, our umpire, called.

"Pay attention to *this* game, Rufus," Jeff said, sounding disgusted.

My teammates took up a chant. "Hit, hit, hit, hit."

I turned just as Big Douggie fouled a ball off to the side.

"Strike two!" Mrs. Mattingly called out.

"Hit, hit, hit, hit."

My head was pounding. My heart was going double-time. Not even a wizard could hit a ball and cast a spell at the same time. Especially not with that racket going on.

The ball came toward me. Without thinking, I swung with all my might and sent the ball deep in the outfield.

"Run, Run!" Jeff screamed.

I ran around the bases. Someone yelled "keep going," so I did. I reached home a nanosecond before the ball came whizzing by.

"Home run! Yeah!" Jeff shouted, punching his hands in the air.

My teammates surrounded me. They patted and pounded me. Hildegarde and Billy ran over to congratulate me.

"Nice hit, Rufus," Billy said. He lowered his voice to a whisper, "Was that you or the magic?"

"Me, you idiot! Do you think I'd waste magic on this dumb game?"

"Congratulations, Rufus. You probably just made the All-Star Game," Jeff said in his know-it-all voice.

"The All-Star Game?" I echoed foolishly.

"Don't pretend you didn't know today were the tryouts," Jeff said.

I shrugged. "Of course I knew. Didn't everyone?"

A whistle screeched. "PLAY BALL!"Mr. Carstairs ordered.

Play ball! In all the excitement, I'd forgotten about Big Douggie. I shivered. Wizard or no wizard, I dreaded to think of what Big Douggie would do to me if he struck out.

I was lucky. All the noise because of my home run had stopped their game. Like us, they were first getting back to play.

I waved at Big Douggie to get his attention. When he turned to me, I was sorry I did. His eyes were a fiery red, like the eyes of an enraged bull. What was he so angry about? Jealous was more like it. I covered my mouth to hide my grin. Big Douggie was jealous of my home run!

I sent him a mental message—Relax. Your double is coming in on the next pitch. I decided to go for magnanimous. I'll make it a home run, I told him.

Suddenly Big Douggie was all smiles. He tipped his baseball cap in my direction. Then he took up his stance at the mound. The pitch came. He connected. The rest is history.

The loud noise told me I'd done something awful. That was no softball sound. It was more like an explosion. A rocket taking off for the moon. Everyone stared as the ball sailed high, high, even higher into the sky.

"Wow, Look at it go!" Jeff shouted and pointed. The ball arced over the playground and headed for the building.

"It's going to crash through a window!" someone yelled.

Which is exactly what it did. It smashed through *our* classroom window on the second floor.

I felt sick. I wanted to disappear into the clear spring air. A dreamy sensation came over me. I knew I'd start to fade if I didn't make a conscious effort to pull back into the here and now.

Billy poked me with his elbow. "Awesome, Rufus," he said. "That even tops the fire drill."

I covered my face with my hands. "I'm going home. I'm too dangerous to stay in school."

"Oh, oh," Billy said. "Come on." He started to run, pulling me along.

I turned. Big Douggie had circled the bases. Now he

was bearing down on us, his nostrils flaring like a raging bull's. Was it my imagination, or were they giving off steam?

"I'll get you for this, Rufus! Don't think I won't!"

Mr. Carstairs and another coach tackled Big Douggie. All three fell down in a heap. I made a beeline for Mrs. Mattingly. I threw myself down at her feet.

"Mrs. Mattingly," I said, between gasps for breath, "I set off the fire alarm and made the floods and broke the window just now. I'm sorry, really sorry. I promise I won't ever do it again."

Chapter Eleven

Mrs. Mattingly took me to the nurse's office. She sat beside me while the nurse gave me a drink of water and put a blanket around my shoulder so I wouldn't get chilled. Get chilled! Get real, I thought. It was warm out. Warm enough for kids to be wearing shorts.

The nurse and Mrs. Mattingly whispered together, then the nurse made a phone call. I saw her shake her head.

"My mom's away," I offered. "My dad's in his office in the city. Don't call him, *please*!"

They went back to whispering. Then another phone call. "It's all arranged," the nurse announced.

"What's all arranged?" I asked.

Instead of answering, Mrs. Mattingly gave me the kind of smile a parent gives a kid who comes down with chicken pox the first day of spring vacation.

"Feel better, Rufus. I'll see you tomorrow."

I jumped to my feet. "I feel fine," I insisted. "I can come to class with you."

The nurse gently pushed me back in the chair. "You can go to class tomorrow, Rufus. Today I want you to talk to someone."

The someone turned out to be Dr. Polchark, the school psychologist. She was young and pretty and nice. She had a nice office, too. I sank back in the plushy arm-chair while Dr. Polchark chatted on in a real friendly way. She said she'd been working in the school for two whole years and she was finally getting the chance to talk to me. She knew I was smart and got good grades, then she asked if I had any special interests. Sure, collecting comic books, I told her. She wanted to know how I got along with Griselda. And if I had any friends.

I explained that Billy was my best friend and I'd probably be going to the South of France with him and his parents.

Then she asked me about Big Douggie.

I told Dr. Polchark Big Douggie used to chase me home from school. He bullied and teased me, and I was afraid of him until a while ago.

"What happened then, Rufus?" Dr. Polchark asked. Her eyes turned watchful.

I knew Dr. Polchark wanted to help me, so I gave her the truth. I explained how I made Big Douggie do a somersault, so he started bothering Hildegarde instead. But in order to protect Hildegarde and my secret, I promised him a double. Only *that* got all screwed up when I turned it into a home run."

Dr. Polchark's eyes opened as wide as they could go.

Since she didn't tell me to stop, I continued.

"I never meant to set off the sprinkler system, or to make Big Douggie break the window. My parents are going to be furious when they find out. I'm new at this witch—I mean, wizard, business," I explained. And quickly added, "Please don't tell anyone about my powers. Only Billy and Hildegarde and Big Douggie know. And they won't say a word."

Dr. Polchark got up and stood beside me. She put her hand on my shoulder. It was shaking.

"Rufus?"

"Hmmm?"

"Mrs. Mattingly told me you hit a home run in gym today."

"I sure did!" I said, excited. "No magic about that."

Dr. Polchark gave me a big smile. Like I'd just passed some important test I didn't know I was taking. "Exactly, Rufus. It was a real, authentic home run. I'm sure you feel good about it."

I shrugged. "Sure. Fine."

"That's something you did on your own. You earned it."

She started pacing the floor, not looking at me. "But the other incidents were things you *think* you did. To give you a sense of power. Over situations and people you feel you can't control. Like the sprinkler system. Did you know that it went off last night?"

I shook my head.

"Well it did. There's something wrong with the sensor. They're fixing it this afternoon."

"But I set off the alarm—" I began. Dr. Polchark interrupted with a shake of her head.

"You *didn't*, Rufus. You only think you did." She paused. "As for Douglas, sometimes when people aren't nice to us, we imagine ways to deal with them." Dr. Polchark cleared her throat. "Do you understand what I mean, Rufus?"

I understood all right! Dr. Polchark thought I was crazy. Bonkers! That I was living in a fantasy world. For people like her, there were no wizards. There was no magic.

I nodded. "I know what you mean, Dr. Polchark."

Dr. Polchark smiled. "Good, Rufus. When your mother comes home, we'll have a little talk. I want you to see someone who can help you."

"Sure, Dr. Polchark. I know I can use some help."

I was thinking of lessons with Mom, but Dr. Polchark didn't know that. She didn't know lots of things, but she meant well.

She gave me a broad grin, and said, "I just might be able to dig up some comic books. Why don't you read them till it's time to go home."

"Cool! I can't think of anything better."

Dr. Polchark's pile of comic books was awesome. She had some old Supermans, Captain Marvels, and Archies. I leafed through them and wondered if she knew what they were worth. I wondered if she'd be willing to sell me a few.

I was still reading when the dismissal bell rang.

"Time to go home, Rufus." Dr. Polchark took the comics from me.

"Right," I said, then added what Mom had taught me to say when I'd been invited to someone's home. "And thank you for having me."

That made Dr. Polchark laugh. "It was a pleasure meeting you, Rufus. Please come and talk whenever something's troubling you."

"Sure thing," I said, though I knew I'd never come back.

I picked up my bookbag, which Billy had brought down, and started for home. I thought as I walked. Slowly, because I had plenty to think about.

Like how great it had been to catch a fly and hit a home run instead of flubbing things as usual.

And how lucky I'd been that no one in school believed I was responsible for the fire drill and the broken window.

I suddenly thought of Mom and realized she wasn't going to stop me from doing *all* magic. I had to cast spells in order to learn, right? I grinned as I got the very definite feeling that now that I'd be taking witch lessons, she'd let me go to France.

I wondered how I could get Dad to tell me more about Uncle Hector without driving him berserk. Now *that* required some serious planning.

A huge mitt of a hand grabbed my upper arm and spun me around.

Big Douggie loomed over me. He grinned his squinty-eyed grin. "Hey, Rufus. I want to talk to you."

Sure you do. I lowered my head and, using it as a battering ram, slammed deep into Big Douggie's stomach.

A solid hit. Big Douggie sank to the ground. He sat there, his mouth open wide enough to catch flies.

"Hey, Rufus," he complained. "What did you do that for?"

I felt strong. Powerful. I bent down till my face was inches from his. "Touch me again, and you'll know all about the life of an amphibian. First hand."

"What's an amphibian?" Big Douggie asked, rubbing his stomach.

"A frog! Geez! Don't you know anything?"

"Oh."

Big Douggie lumbered to his feet. I stepped back.

"Just keep away from me, okay?" I said. "I'm sorry

the home run didn't work out. I didn't mean to get you into trouble. I tried explaining it to Dr. Polchark, but she thinks I'm hallucinating."

I looked over to see how Big Douggie was taking all this in. He had a huge grin on his face.

"Take it easy, Rufus. Everything worked out fine." Big Douggie rubbed his right arm. "The Coach thinks I have a great arm. And you know what, Rufus? I get the feeling I won't have any more trouble in that department."

"Great. And I'm glad you're not mad." I started walking away.

Big Douggie walked beside me. "Of course I'm not mad, Rufus. I'm grateful. Really grateful."

I squirmed. I didn't like having Douggie *grateful*. "Fine," I said. "As long as you understand, Douggie. No more favors. And you leave Hildegarde alone, like we agreed."

"Sure," Douggie said, and kept on walking.

I walked faster. Douggie kept pace. I ran. Douggie ran, too. We went on like this for half a block, then he let out his dumb, high laugh. "So Dr. Polchark thought you were hallucinating, huh?"

I slowed down. I was kind of surprised he knew what "hallucinating" meant. "She doesn't believe there are such things as magic and wizards."

"Yeah," Big Douggie said, "But she sure has the greatest comics."

I stared at Douggie. There was only one way he could know *that*. I gave him a meaningful look. "You keep my secret, and I'll keep yours."

"Right." Douggie stretched out his hand. I had no choice but to shake it.

Too late, I realized Douggie had suckered me in. He wanted me to know he saw Dr. Polchark. He got me to say I'd keep my mouth shut about it all on my own. Just as I, Rufus Breckenridge, should have known he'd never tell anyone I was responsible for his amazing hit. I shook my head. In some ways, Big Douggie was smarter than me.

We started walking. "Hey, Rufus," Douggie said. "I've been thinking."

I shuddered. "About what?"

He smiled. "You turned out to be an all-right guy. You helped me with my little problem. I think I can help you with yours."

"What problem are you talking about?"

"Well," Douggie began, "since we'll both be playing in the All-Star Game—"

I grabbed his arm. "Wait a minute. I made the All-Star Game?"

"Didn't anyone tell you? The Coach came around with the list just before the bell rang."

I threw my bookbag in the air. "I made the All-Star Game! I made the All-Star Game!"

"Stop acting so surprised," Douggie said, disgusted. "You used enough magic to light up a Christmas tree."

I looked up at him. "But I didn't use any magic. I did it all by myself."

That stunned him. He shook his head. He spun in circles. "Wow! That's unreal." Douggie squinted down at me. "I can't believe you're the same little twerp I used to chase home every other day."

"That's because I'm not the same person," I said.

Big Douggie threw his arm around my shoulders. "You got that right, Rufus. Now you have heart. Now you and me can be friends."

My head began to throb. I didn't like the way this conversation was going. "Friends?" I echoed.

"Right, friends." Big Douggie grinned. "And I'll show you what a good friend I can be."

I was too shocked to say one word.

"Now don't take this wrong, Rufus, but what you know about playing ball, you can write on a stick of gum. As your good friend, I'd like to give you some pointers. How about this afternoon?"

I thought wildly for some excuse. "I don't know, Douggie. I have to walk my dog, Spots."

"And then?"

I cleared my throat. "Then I usually do something with Billy."

"So? Billy can come along." He squeezed my shoulder. "How about if I stop by in an hour. Then you, me, and Billy can go out to the field behind the school?"

I shrugged. "I guess."

"Great! I'll bring the bat and ball."

I watched him disappear down the block. Big Douggie had gone from being my bully to my buddy. Frankly, it wasn't much of an improvement.

My head tingled. I considered making Big Douggie disappear for good. Only I couldn't. Then I'd be as bad as Uncle Hector. I was going to have to solve the Big Douggie Problem by myself.

I supposed there were worse things in the world. Only right now I couldn't think what one could be.

Hey, hey, enough of this gloom and doom! A new force inside me—a force that had nothing to do with magic—thrust back my shoulders and had me walking tall. I wasn't a twerp, and I'd better not think like a twerp. I, Rufus Breckenridge, had pride. I had self-respect. I was an all-right, average American boy.

I grinned as I crossed the street. Actually, I was better

than average. I'd made the All-Star Game, hadn't I? And I was tough enough to ram Big Douggie smack in the gut. I'd managed to ditch my fears, and I did it all on my own!

A shiver ran down my back as it hit me the reason I'd played so well today was because I'd been distracted. Nothing was bound to distract me the day of the All-Star Game. I'd be scared and nervous, with hundreds of eyes watching me. Waiting to see me connect—or strike out.

I'd strike out, all right, unless I used magic. But I didn't *want* to use magic. Not for something I'd earned on my own.

I sighed as I realized Douggie was right. If I hoped to play well in the game, I desperately needed his pointers. In fact, I desperately needed as much practice time as he was willing to spare. I shook my head at the incredible idea that I, Rufus Breckenridge, was about to ask Big Douggie for help. Billy would laugh over this one *for weeks*.

My head started to tingle as I got near our house. The old magic was stirring. Sure, I wasn't supposed to do anything, but why waste perfectly good magical energy? I tossed my bookbag in the air and watch it circle once, twice, three times before it drifted down to my feet.

I took the stairs slowly, wondering how it felt to walk on air. I wouldn't try it, not yet. But I was a wizard, and one day I would. I'd take Mom's old lessons and read Grandma's book, but sooner or later, I was going to use my powers to the hilt. And then world, watch out!